When the Wind Bears Go Dancing

Written and illustrated by
Phoebe Stone

Little, Brown and Company

BOSTON   NEW YORK   LONDON

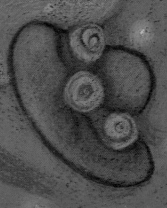

When it's time for bed and a storm's coming soon,
I look up at the clouds and the dark howling moon.
When I'm scared of the thunder and wind in the sky,
My mommy says, "Listen! It's the bears dancing by!
See them razzle and dazzle? Hear them rumble and roam?
When the Wind Bears go dancing, *you'd* better stay home!"

When the Wind Bears go dancing, I might go along,
Though my mommy says, "No, dear. That *really* seems wrong.
Those bears are so curly and woolly and wild . . .
They're too fuzzy and frisky for such a small child!"

When the Wind Bears go dancing, I, too, want to go.
We'll wear coats and big hats so that no one will know
Just how woolly and windy and silly we are
When we're racing around in a rattle-bang car.
We boom and we zoom and we whistle and fly!
When the Wind Bears go dancing, we romp through the sky.

When the Wind Bears go dancing, we romp through the night
And we giggle and wiggle in orange moonlight
And we rumble and tumble and spin and we twirl....

We're just five woolly Wind Bears and one little girl!

We dance on the rooftops and we dance in the eaves,
We flip-flop the shutters and rustle the leaves.
One of the bears hangs up high by his toes.
The wider he swings, the more the wind blows.

When the Wind Bears go dancing, not a thing can sit still —
Fish leap from the water, grass rolls on the hill.
Everything dances and sings a refrain. . . .
When the bears shake their coats, down comes the rain.

When the Wind Bears go dancing, I, too, sing along
As the stormy night band plays a rainy wind song.
Tigers with tambourines jump on the ground,
Drumming up thunder and crashing around.
A bear tickles a tiger, who laughs as he flies —
His laughter's the lightning that zigzags the skies.

Then the lions and leopards and lynx play the strings.
Hear them howling and yowling the way the wind sings.

One big curly bear plays a great wind bassoon,
And we hum and we strum and we shimmy and swoon.
The rain sings the chorus. Leaves shiver and blow.
When the Wind Bears make music, the storm starts to grow.

Then we climb in the car and we roar through the sky
And the people below say, "The wind's passing by!"
They rush to their windows to look at the storm,
Feeling happy and safe and protected and warm.

When the Wind Bears get sleepy, one bear takes a bow,
Calls out to the wind, *"It's time for bed now!"*
First the bears, then the tigers curl up in the trees,
And the wind quiets down to a gentle, soft breeze.

Then late in the night and long before day,
The trees full of Wind Bears float off and away.

When I look out my window, up at the sky,
My Wind Bears are the storm clouds waving good-bye.

When the Wind Bears go dancing, if Mommy says, "No,"
You can still dream of Wind Bears as stormy winds blow.
If you're feeling unsleepy and you just can't count sheep . . .
Listen. Listen to the wind and you'll drift off to sleep.